THIS WALKER BOOK BELONGS TO:

_____

_____

_____

_____

To Fintan
from us both

First published 1995 by Walker Books Ltd
87 Vauxhall Walk, London SE11 5HJ

This edition published 2001

2 4 6 8 10 9 7 5 3 1

Text © 1995 Martin Waddell
Illustrations © 1995 Leo Hartas

The right of Martin Waddell to be identified as author
of this work has been asserted by him in accordance with
the Copyright, Designs and Patents Act 1988

Printed in Hong Kong

British Library Cataloguing in Publication Data:
a catalogue record for this book
is available from the British Library

ISBN 0-7445-8274-1

Mimi
and the
Dream House

Written by
MARTIN WADDELL
Illustrated by
LEO HARTAS

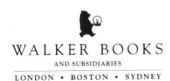

WALKER BOOKS
AND SUBSIDIARIES
LONDON · BOSTON · SYDNEY

Mimi lived with her mouse sisters
and brothers in their mouse-house
beneath the big tree.

"This house is too small," Mimi decided.
"I want a mouse-house where
I can be me!"
And she sat down and
thought about how
it might be.

Mimi drew her Dream House.
She called it *Chez Mouse* and
she told her mouse sisters
about it.

"That's brilliant, Mimi!" her mouse
sisters cried. "We'll build it for you!"

They worked …

and they worked …

and they worked …

and they worked …

and they worked …

and they worked …

adding bits that they'd thought of themselves.

This is the house that the mouse sisters built. "Thank you so much!" Mimi said. "It's a very nice house … but it isn't *Chez Mouse*. Can't you see? I want a mouse-house where I can be me!"

Mimi drew a new picture of her
Dream House.
"I call it *Chez Mouse*," she told
her mouse brothers.

"It looks lovely, Mimi!" her mouse
brothers said, clapping their paws.
"We'll build it for you!"

They worked …

and they worked …

and they worked …

and they worked …

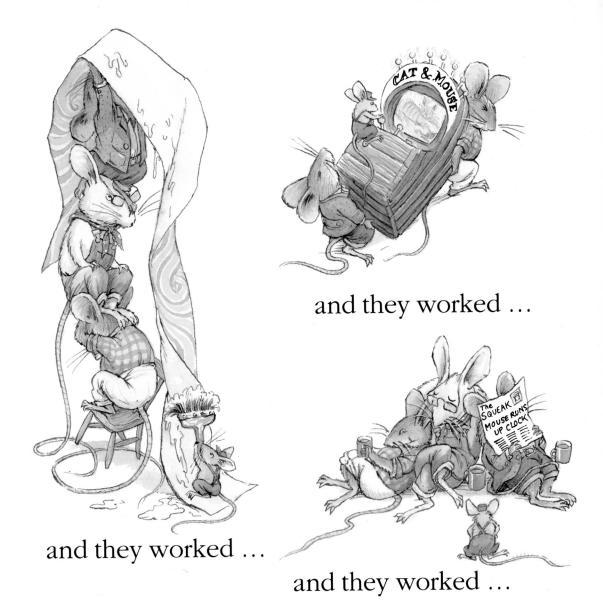

and they worked …

and they worked …

and they worked …

adding bits that they'd thought of themselves.

This is the house that the mouse brothers built.
"You've all been so good," Mimi said.
"It's a very nice house … but it isn't
Chez Mouse. Can't you see? I want a
mouse-house where I can be me!"

And she sat down again and thought
about how it might be.

"This time I'll build it myself!" Mimi said.
So she drew her Dream House once
again and then…

She worked …

and she worked …

and she worked …

and she worked …

and she worked …

and she worked…

And she built her Dream House, all by herself!

This is *Chez Mouse*, Mimi's Dream
House that she built by herself.
"This is my mouse-house where I
can be me!" Mimi said.
"You must come and see!"

And her sisters and brothers …

all came to tea!

MARTIN WADDELL was inspired to write **Mimi and the Dream House** by his neighbour, Liz. "She was so excited about her building plans that her enthusiasm bubbled its way into my brain," he says. "She became Mimi, and that is why the book is dedicated to her."

Martin Waddell is widely regarded as one of the finest contemporary writers of books for young people. Twice Winner of the Smarties Book Prize – for *Farmer Duck* and *Can't You Sleep, Little Bear?* – he also won the Kurt Maschler Award for *The Park in the Dark* and the Best Books for Babies Award for *Rosie's Babies*. Among his many other titles are *Owl Babies*; *Night Night, Cuddly Bear* and three other stories about Mimi. He was the Irish nominee for the 2000 Hans Christian Andersen Award. He lives with his wife Rosaleen in County Down, Northern Ireland.

LEO HARTAS says, "I think that if I were Mimi I'd have liked living with my brothers and sisters as they do at the beginning of the book. It looks so cosy and happy – but perhaps poor Mimi needed some time to herself, as we all do."

Leo Hartas has illustrated over twenty books, including the three other Mimi stories. He taught himself computer graphics and animation and now has a small company working on new ideas for interactive television and the Internet. Of his work he says, "All I have ever done has been because I enjoy it but I'm delighted to find children enjoy it too!" Leo lives in Brighton with his wife and three children.

Other Mimi stories by Martin Waddell and Leo Hartas

Mimi and the Picnic 0-7445-8275-X (p/b) £3.99
Mimi and the Blackberry Pies 0-7445-8279-2 (p/b) £3.99
Mimi's Christmas 0-7445-7213-4 (p/b) £4.99